I Love Christmas

A Wonderful Collection of Christmas Stories, Poems, Carols, and More

Compiled by Walter Retan
Illustrated by Caroline Ewing

For Bud and Evelyne Johnson—C. E.

A GOLDEN BOOK • NEW YORK
Western Publishing Company, Inc., Racine, Wisconsin 53404

© 1992, 1990, 1977, 1976, 1974, 1969, 1950, 1947, 1942 Western Publishing Company, Inc. Illustrations © 1992 Caroline Ewing. Musical arrangement for "Good King Wenceslas" from FAVORITE CHRISTMAS CAROLS reprinted by permission of Simon and Schuster, Inc., © 1957 Simon and Schuster, Inc., and Artists and Writers Guild, Inc. "O Christmas Tree" and "Christmas Stockings" by Kathryn Jackson reprinted by permission of McIntosh and Otis, Inc. All rights reserved. Printed in the U.S.A. No part of this book may be reproduced or copied in any form without written permission from the publisher. All trademarks are the property of Western Publishing Company, Inc. Library of Congress Catalog Card Number: 92-71028 ISBN: 0-307-15875-6/ISBN: 0-307-65875-9 (lib. bdg.)
A MCMXCII

Acknowledgments

The editor and publisher have made every effort to trace the ownership of all copyrighted material and to secure permission from copyright holders. Any errors or omissions are inadvertent, and the publisher will be pleased to make the necessary corrections in future printings. Thanks to the following authors, publishers, and agents for permission to use the material indicated:

Doubleday, a division of Bantam Doubleday Dell Publishing Group, Inc., for "The Christmas Spider" from UP THE HILL by Marguerite de Angeli. Copyright 1942 by Marguerite de Angeli. Used by permission of Doubleday, a division of Bantam Doubleday Dell Publishing Group, Inc.

Harcourt Brace Jovanovich, Inc., for an excerpt abridged from "A Miserable, Merry Christmas" in AUTOBIOGRAPHY OF LINCOLN STEFFENS by Lincoln Steffens, copyright 1931 by Harcourt Brace Jovanovich, Inc., and renewed 1959 by Peter Steffens, reprinted by permission of the publisher.

HarperCollins Publishers for text of "Mrs. Goose's Wild Christmas" from MRS. GOOSE AND THREE-DUCKS by Miriam Clark Potter. Copyright © 1964, 1936 by Miriam Clark Potter. Reprinted by permission of HarperCollins Publishers.

Alfred A. Knopf, Inc., for "December" from A CHILD'S CALENDAR by John Updike. Copyright © 1965 by John Updike and Nancy Burkert. Reprinted by permission of Alfred A. Knopf, Inc.

William Morrow & Company, Inc., for "It's Christmas" by Jack Prelutsky, © 1981 Jack Prelutsky. Used by permission of William Morrow & Company, Inc./Publishers, New York.

Viking Penguin, a division of Penguin Books USA Inc., for "Christmas Eve on the Battlefront" from THE SINGING TREE by Kate Seredy. Copyright 1939 by Kate Seredy, renewed © 1966 by Kate Seredy. Used by permission of Viking Penguin, a division of Penguin Books USA Inc.

Contents

PART ONE

Getting Ready for Christmas

It's Christmas, a poem by Jack Prelutsky   8
The Christmas Tree Lamb, a story by Kathryn Jackson   10
December, a poem by John Updike   14
The Colors of Christmas, facts about the holiday   15
Deck the Halls   16
In the Great Walled Country, a story by Raymond MacDonald Alden   18

PART TWO

The Animals' Christmas

A Very Small Christmas, a poem by Kathryn Jackson   26
Christmas Is for Everyone, a story by Gertrude Crampton   28
Mrs. Goose's Wild Christmas, a story by Miriam Potter   30
The Friendly Beasts, medieval verses   40
Christmas Underground, a story by Kenneth Grahame   42

PART THREE

The Story of the Christ Child

What Can I Give Him? a poem by Christina Rossetti   52
The Birth of Jesus, the Nativity story   54
O Little Town of Bethlehem   56
The Christmas Spider, a Polish folktale retold by Marguerite de Angeli   58
The Visit of the Wise Men, from the New Testament   62
We Three Kings of Orient Are   64
La Befana, a Christmas legend from Italy   66
The Inn That Missed Its Chance, a poem by Amos Russel Wells   68

PART FOUR

The Wonder of Christmas Past

New England, a poem by Phyllis McGinley   70
Christmas Eve on the Battlefront, a story by Kate Seredy   72
Good King Wenceslas   76
O Christmas Tree! a Christmas piece by Kathryn Jackson   78
Christmas Stockings, holiday facts by Kathryn Jackson   79
A Miserable, Merry Christmas, a story by Lincoln Steffens   80
A Visit From Saint Nicholas, a poem by Clement C. Moore   90

It's Christmas

It's Christmas! Merry Christmas!
Yes, it's merry, merry Christmas,
it's a time for hanging stockings,
it's a time for riding sleighs,
it's a time for jolly greeting,
snow and holly, overeating,
oh, I love you merry Christmas,
you're the best of holidays.

—*Jack Prelutsky*

PART ONE
Getting Ready for Christmas

The Christmas Tree Lamb

Once upon a time there was a small white Christmas tree lamb. He belonged to a grandmother when she was a little girl. He belonged to a mother, too, when she was small.

When he belonged to the grandmother, he was a brand-new lamb. His fleece was snowy white against the dark branches of the tree. His black bead eyes shone with lights and excitement. His shining hooves looked as if he might frolic from branch to branch the very next minute.

Besides all that, the tiny golden bell on his collar jingled merrily whenever anyone brushed against the tree.

That was splendid, that first Christmas!

The lamb was new, and the grandmother was little. Everyone said, "The lamb is the prettiest thing on the whole tree!"

There were lots of splendid Christmases.

But after a while the lamb began to look dusty. After a while the grandmother was grown up. Then the Christmas lamb belonged to the mother.

She loved that lamb when she was little. She played with him every year before she put him on the tree.

And one year—*pop!*—one bead eye came loose and rolled into a corner.

The next year—*crack!*—the Christmas lamb lost a leg.

Three years later his tiny golden bell fell off, and it was lost with the lost things of Christmas.

By the time the mother was grown up and had a little girl of her own, that lamb was in a sorry state!

He was gray with dust, and he had only one eye, two legs, no collar, and, of course, no bell! But he was still a Christmas lamb, eagerly waiting to go on the tree.

The grandmother picked him up and said, "We can't put him on the tree anymore!"

The mother took him and said, "No, he's nothing to look at now. But how pretty he was, long ago!"

Now, the little girl reached out her hands for the lamb.

"How did he look?" she asked.

The grandmother told about his snowy white fleece.

The mother told about the golden bell that had jingled so merrily.

And the little girl could see for herself that a lamb should have *two* black eyes and *four* shining hooves.

So she took the lamb into her own room. She brushed and cleaned him until he was as white as the snow falling outside. She made him two new legs and glued them on, then painted the hooves shining black. She sewed a small black bead in place for an eye.

And she tied a bit of red ribbon around the snowy lamb's neck with a new little golden bell in front.

When Christmas Eve came, the little girl crept downstairs with the lamb held behind her back.

She waited until the grandmother wasn't looking.

She waited until the mother wasn't looking.

Then she stood on a chair and put the lamb on the Christmas tree, up near the top, right under the shining star.

When the grandmother saw the lamb, her eyes glistened. "He looks just as he did when I was a little girl," she said in a whisper.

The mother looked then, and her eyes sparkled.

"He looks much finer than he did when I was little!" she said.

The little girl didn't say a word.

She was too busy loving the lamb and thinking he was the prettiest thing on the tree. She touched the tree, and the lamb swayed to and fro. His two eyes shone with lights and excitement. His four hooves looked ready to caper from branch to branch.

And his new golden bell jingled more merrily than the old one ever had. Perhaps that was because the small white Christmas tree lamb was happier than he had ever been in all his white cotton years on all the Christmas trees!

—*Kathryn Jackson*

December

First snow! The flakes
   So few, so light,
Remake the world
   In solid white.

All bundled up,
   We feel as if
We were fat penguins,
   Warm and stiff.

Downtown, the stores
   Half split their sides,
And Mother brings home
   Things she hides.

Old carols peal.
   The dusk is dense.
There is a mood
   Of sweet suspense.

The shepherds wait,
   The kings, the tree—
All wait for something
   Yet to be,

Some miracle.
   And then it's here,
Wrapped up in hope—
   Another year!

—John Updike

The Colors of Christmas

Think of Christmas and what colors do you see?

GREEN for the fresh-smelling evergreen trees that people bring into their homes. Green, too, for the wreaths they hang in their doorways and windows. Green is the symbol of nature, youth (the Christ child), and hope.

RED is another important color of the holiday season. Santa Claus wears a suit of red. The tiny berries on the holly branches used to decorate wreaths and windows are also red. And the bright-red poinsettia is the traditional Christmas flower. Red is the symbol of family (blood), love, and charity.

WHITE is the color of snow, which everyone longs to see at Christmastime. It is also the color of Santa's beard. Christmas angels have shimmering white wings and robes. The color white symbolizes purity, light, and joy.

GOLD stands for the glowing flames of Christmas candles, twinkling Christmas lights, and the glow from the Yule log burning in fireplaces. Gold is the symbol of sunlight and radiance.

SILVER represents the color of the stars that twinkle at the top of the Christmas tree, and the long strings of tinsel that wind around it. Silver symbolizes giving and wealth.

Truly, Christmas is a time of strong, bright colors and good cheer.

Deck the Halls

*One of the gayest and best-liked of any of the secular Christmas carols.
The tune was used by Mozart in the eighteenth century
in a set of variations for the violin and piano.*

Traditional Welsh Melody
With Spirit

Words Traditional

1. Deck the halls with boughs of hol-ly,⟩
2. See the blaz-ing Yule be-fore us,⟩ Fa, la, la, la, la, la, la, la, la.
3. Fast a-way the old year pass-es,⟩

'Tis the sea-son to be jol-ly,⟩
Strike the harp and join the cho-rus,⟩ Fa, la, la, la, la, la, la, la, la.
Hail the new, ye lads and lass-es,⟩

Don we now our gay ap-par-el,⟩
Fol-low me in mer-ry meas-ure,⟩ Fa, la, la, la, la, la, la, la, la.
Sing we joy-ous all to-geth-er,⟩

Troll the an-cient Yule-tide car-ol,⟩
While I tell of Yule-tide treas-ure,⟩ Fa, la, la, la, la, la, la, la, la.
Heed-less of the wind and weath-er,⟩

In the Great Walled Country

The story that follows was written in 1906 by Raymond MacDonald Alden. It was one of a collection of enchanting tales entitled Why the Chimes Ring and Other Stories. *The author was a distinguished American university professor. Today his name lives on because a poetic imagination and pure, simple style made him a master at the art of writing romantic parables for young readers.*

Away at the northern end of the world is a land full of children, called the Great Walled Country. All around the country is a great wall, hundreds of feet thick and hundreds of feet high. It is made of ice that never melts. That's why very few people have ever discovered the place.

Grandfather Christmas lives just to the north of the country. In fact, his house leans right against the great wall. (We call him Santa Claus, but in the Great Walled Country he is called Grandfather Christmas.) One very pleasant thing about having Grandfather Christmas for a neighbor is that the people in the Great Walled Country never have to buy Christmas presents. Every year, on the day before Christmas, Grandfather Christmas goes into the great forest of Christmas trees behind the king's palace and fills the trees with candy, books, toys, and all sorts of good things. When night comes, all the children wrap up snugly and go to the forest to gather gifts for their friends. Each one goes alone so that no one can see what the others have gathered. They never think of taking presents for themselves.

But there was one time, many years ago, when the children in the Great Walled Country had a very different kind of Christmas. A visitor had come to the land—an old man. He was the first stranger for many years who had succeeded in getting over the wall.

When this old man was told how they celebrated Christmas, he said to the king, "That is all very well, but I think that children who have Grandfather Christmas for a neighbor could find a better way. Why not go out together, and everyone get his own presents? Then everybody would be better satisfied."

This seemed to the king to be a very wise suggestion, and his courtiers and counselors all agreed. "We will make a proclamation," they said, "and from now on everybody will follow the new plan."

The plan seemed as wise to the children as to the king and the counselors. Everyone had at sometime been a little disappointed with his Christmas gifts.

But one person at the palace was not at all pleased with the new proclamation. This was a little boy named Inge, who lived with his sister. His sister's legs were not strong enough for walking, so she had to sit all day looking out of the window from her chair. He had always gone to the forest on Christmas Eve and returned with arms and pockets loaded with pretty things for her.

But now, thought Inge, what would she do? After thinking about it a long time, he made up his mind not to obey the proclamation. He decided it would not be wrong if, instead of taking gifts for himself, he took them for his sister.

As soon as the chimes struck ten, the children made their way toward the forest in starlight so bright that it showed their shadows on the sparkling snow. When they came to the edge of the forest, they separated.

Ten minutes later, if you had been in the forest, you would have seen the children standing in dismay with tears on their faces. They had found nothing hanging from the low-bending branches of the evergreen trees that could not be seen every day in the year. High and low they searched, wandering farther into the forest than ever before. But still no presents appeared.

As the children came trooping out of the forest, after hours of weary searching, they met little Inge. He was carrying a bag full to overflowing. "Are they not beautiful things?" he cried. "Grandfather Christmas was never so good to us before."

"What do you mean?" asked the children. "There are no presents in the forest."

"No presents!" said Inge. "I have a bag full of them." But he didn't offer to show the presents, because he didn't want the children to see that they were all for his little sister.

When the children begged him to tell them where he had found his presents, he turned back, pointing to the place in the forest where he had been. "I left many more behind than I brought away," he said. "I can see some shining on the trees even from here."

But when the children followed his footprints in the snow to the place where he had been, they still saw nothing on the trees. They thought that Inge must be dreaming. Perhaps he had filled his bag with pine cones.

On Christmas Day there was sadness all through the Great Walled Country. But those who visited the house of Inge and his sister saw plenty of books and dolls and beautiful toys piled about the little girl's chair. When they asked where these things came from, Inge said, "Why, from the Christmas tree forest."

The king held a meeting and appointed a committee to visit Grandfather Christmas to see what was the matter. The committee had a very hard time climbing the great wall of ice, but at last they reached the top. And when they came to the other side of the wall, they could look straight down into the top of Grandfather Christmas's chimney. It was not hard to go down this chimney, and at the bottom of it they found themselves in the very room where Grandfather Christmas lay sound asleep.

It was difficult to awaken him, as he always slept for one hundred days after his Christmas work was over. But at last Grandfather Christmas sat up in bed, rubbing his eyes.

"Oh, sir!" cried the prince, who was in charge of the committee. "We have come from the king of the Great Walled Country to ask why you forgot us this Christmas and left no presents in the forest."

"No presents!" said Grandfather Christmas. "The presents were there. You must not have seen them, that's all."

But the children told him that they had searched carefully, and in the whole forest they had not found a single Christmas gift.

"Indeed!" said Grandfather Christmas. "And did little Inge find none for his sister?"

The committee was silent. They had heard of the gifts at Inge's house and didn't know what to say.

"You had better go home," said Grandfather Christmas, "and let me finish my nap. The presents were there, but they were never intended for children who were looking only for gifts for themselves. I'm not surprised that you couldn't see them. Remember that not everything that strange travelers tell you is wise." And he turned over and went to sleep again.

The committee returned silently to the Great Walled Country and told the king what they had found out. When next December came, he made another proclamation, bidding everyone to seek gifts for others, in the old way, in the Christmas tree forest. And that is what they have been doing ever since.

—*Raymond MacDonald Alden*

A Very Small Christmas

I wonder if the chipmunks know,
  When everything is white with snow
And night starts coming very fast,
  That Christmastime is here at last?

And do the little chipmunks go
  To sleep, quite early, in a row—
With Christmas dreams inside their heads
  And extra blankets on their beds?

And do they hop up just at dawn
  And put their robes and slippers on
And hurry out to peep and see
  If someone brought a Christmas tree?

If someone did, I wonder who?
  Their chimney's small to wriggle through!
Their Christmas tree must be a twig—
  But maybe chipmunks think it's big.
I hope it's trimmed with sunflower seeds,
  And peanuts, too, and icy beads,
And lighted candles (birthday size)
  To make a grand chipmunk surprise!

—Kathryn Jackson

PART TWO
The Animals' Christmas

Christmas Is for Everyone

Pig wanted a Christmas tree.
But his mother said, "Christmas
isn't for pigs. It's for children."

So he went to see his friend Rabbit.
But Rabbit's mother said, "Christmas
isn't for pigs or rabbits. It's for children."

So they went to see their friend Squirrel.
But Squirrel's mother said,
"Christmas isn't for pigs or rabbits
or squirrels. It's for children."

So they went to see their friend Skunk.
But Skunk's mother said,
"Christmas isn't for pigs or rabbits
or squirrels or skunks. It's for children."

So they went to see their friend Owl.
But all that Owl would say was, "Come
back here Christmas morning."

So Christmas morning they took their mothers and their presents to Owl's tree.

The snow and the frost and the early sun had trimmed Owl's tree so that it looked just as beautiful as any Christmas tree.

"Christmas is for everybody!" said Pig and Rabbit and Squirrel and Skunk and Owl *and* the mothers.

And it is, too.

—Gertrude Crampton

Mrs. Goose's Wild Christmas

One morning in December when Mrs. Goose went to her front door, there was a letter for her. It was written on birch-bark paper, and tied around with green grass ribbon.

Mrs. Goose was so excited that her wings fluttered and trembled. She opened the envelope, sat down in her little rocking chair, and put on her glasses.

The letter was printed in queer, green, wiggly letters. It said:

DEAR MRS. GOOSE,

PLEASE COME AND SPEND CHRISTMAS WITH ME IN MY RIVER HOME. I WILL FLY BY YOU AT FIVE O'CLOCK ON CHRISTMAS EVE. BE READY TO FLY UP AND FLY AWAY WITH ME.

YOUR FLYING COUSIN,
MRS. WILD-GOOSE-OF-THE-MARSHES.

"My, there are a lot of 'flys' in that letter," said Mrs. Goose, blinking. She got up from her rocking chair and said to herself, "I don't believe I know how to fly. I've been a tame goose for so long that I've forgotten."

She thought for a minute, and then she flapped her wings. "No, I haven't forgotten," she told herself.

Three-Ducks were coming over for a cup of hot clover tea at four o'clock. Mrs. Goose kept very busy till they came, tying up presents for her friends. "Don't open till Christmas," she wrote on them. "They can look at them when they have the big Animaltown Christmas Tree party," she planned. "But I won't be here!" Yes, she had decided to spend Christmas with her wild marsh cousin.

At four o'clock, she heard a quacking at the door, and she ran to let Three-Ducks in. "It's getting very cold and blowy," they told her, as they marched over to the fire. "We think it's going to snow," they said, as they warmed their wings.

"I hope it won't snow on Christmas Eve at five o'clock," Mrs. Goose told them. "Because I am going away then."

"*Away?*" quacked Three-Ducks, looking at her.

"Yes, away; I am going to visit my cousin, Mrs. Wild-Goose," and she showed them the birch-bark letter.

"Oh, Mrs. Goose—you won't be here for Christmas—and our big Animaltown party," said Three-Ducks.

"No."

"Why—we'll miss you so much!"

"I'll miss you, too," said Mrs. Goose, getting the teapot.

"And you'll not like the way your cousin lives. She doesn't have a cozy home like yours! She sleeps in a wet river place."

Mrs. Goose poured the tea. "Yes, but she *is* my cousin," she told Three-Ducks. "Our mothers were sister geese. I have decided to go."

They drank their tea, and they talked some more about it, but Three-Ducks couldn't make Mrs. Goose change her mind. She was just determined to go on Christmas Eve; that was all there was about it.

On the day before Christmas, Mrs. Goose was very busy. She tied bright bunches of holly berries on her friends' presents. She packed a little bag with her long gray nightgown and funny white nightcap, and feather-brush.

She swept her house and put it all in order. Then she put on her red shoes and her blue and lavender dress and bright red shawl and hat with parsley on it.

She looked at herself in the glass and said, "There I am. I look very handsome, really—I hope my cousin will be proud of me."

Tap-tap-tap. That was Three-Ducks at the door. They had come to see her off. *Scratch-scratch-scratch.* That was Mrs. Squirrel. Then came Mr. Pig and Mr. Gobbler and the Pop-Rabbits. It was very exciting, coming to see Mrs. Goose fly off—just like waiting to see a balloon go up, or something. "Do you *know* how to fly?" asked Mrs. Squirrel. "Yes, I know," answered Mrs. Goose.

They all went outside to watch for Mrs. Wild-Goose.

The wind made little scurry-tracks in the snow, and there were gray clouds scudding over. "I wish she'd hurry," said Mrs. Goose, drawing her shawl closer around her. "I'm cold."

"I wish you'd change your mind," sighed Mrs. Squirrel. "I hate to think of your flying around loose in the sky somewhere. Don't go!"

"Yes, I'm going," said Mrs. Goose, firmly.

"I don't believe her cousin is coming," Three-Ducks whispered. "It's five minutes past five already."

But just then there was a faraway honking sound. In a minute, a wild goose came into sight. She came nearer and nearer. She flew over Mrs. Goose's chimney.

"There she is—good-by—" said Mrs. Goose, flapping her wings.

But there she stayed, right on the ground.

"Try again," said Three-Ducks.

She flapped and flapped, but she did not rise.

"Take off your clothes!" came a wild voice from the sky. "Throw off your bag! You are toooo heavy!" And there was a sound like laughter, cold laughter, with wind in it.

So Mrs. Goose took off her dress, and her shawl, and her hat, and threw her bag down on the ground. She flapped her wings again, and up she rose, with a great noise. As she rose, she kicked over her red shoes. They fell down and one of them whacked Mr. Pig on the nose.

"Good-by—Mrs. Goose—" Mr. Pig sneezed.

"Good-by," they all called.

"Good-by—" she answered them, as she rose higher and higher.

"There she goes, for her wild Christmas," said Three-Ducks. "I hope she'll have a good time." They gulped hard in their throats, because they missed her already. "We'd better take her things into the house and lock the door, just as she told us to, and put the key under the mat. There she flies—over the pine tree-tops. And there are going to be lots of presents for her at the Christmas party tomorrow—and she won't be here to get them. She said she'd open them when she got back."

"Maybe she won't *get* back," sighed Mrs. Squirrel. "Maybe we'll never see her again." And they all began to cry a little, feeling so sad on Christmas Eve at quarter past five o'clock.

At seven o'clock, when Three-Ducks came back from a little visit at Mrs. Squirrel's house, there was a light shining from Mrs. Goose's window.

"We must go and look in," they said. "Who could be there? Mrs. Goose is away. We must go and see."

So they plopped over and peeked in the window.

There was Mrs. Goose with her wrapper and white nightcap on, warming her wings before the fire.

Tap-tap-tap at the door went Three-Ducks, with excited bills. They were *so* glad!

"Shhhhhh!" said Mrs. Goose, as she let them in. "Yes, I'm back. (Whisper.) Yes, my wings are tired. (*Please* whisper!) For my wild cousin is here—she's in my bed, sleeping. She's come to spend Christmas with me."

"But we thought you were going to spend Christmas with *her*!"

"I did spend two hours with her," said Mrs. Goose. "That was long enough. Yes, you were right, Three-Ducks. Her house is very cold, right by the river. Just frozen rattle reeds, lumps of ice, and wind blowing your

feathers this way and that. One of my best tail feathers blew right out!
She had a few wintergreen berries stuck around; we ate those. 'This is our
Christmas dinner, really,' said my cousin. 'We'll have it today, instead of
tomorrow. We'll spend Christmas flying, my tame cousin. You need
practice. You fly very badly. We'll go far over those snow-covered hills.'"

"How cold and unpleasant," shivered Three-Ducks. "What did you
say?"

"I said—'Now I've had a sort of a Christmas with you—a nice berry
meal—please come back to my house with me, and see what Christmas
there is like. We give presents to each other; we have a party and lots of
dancing and laughing, and try to make each other happy and full of
pleasant feelings.' And do you know—she had never heard of a party in a
house beside a fire. She didn't know about giving presents! Awfully wild,
I think. Well, I talked and talked, and after a while she said she would
come."

"And she's here now—sleeping in your bed?" asked Three-Ducks. "Oh,
do let us have a peek at her, please."

"Will you be very quiet? Will you put your feet down softly, and not quack?"

"Oh, yes; yes."

So Mrs. Goose lit a candle, and they stepped softly to the bedroom. She held the light up high, so they could see better.

But there was no one in the bed!

The covers were thrown back, as though some one had got out quickly, and there was one long feather on the blanket.

"Why—she's *gone*," said Mrs. Goose, looking at the open window.

"She's flown away. You can't be wild, and she can't be tame," said Three-Ducks, wisely.

"Our mothers were sister geese," Mrs. Goose told them. "But *we* don't seem to belong in the same family."

"And you'll be here for the Christmas party, after all," laughed Three-Ducks.

* * * * * * *

And they had the happiest Christmas that they had ever had…. They sang animal songs, and played games, and the refreshments were delicious. The tree was trimmed with little balls of cotton, strings of pink pop-corn, and a few stars and candles.

Mrs. Goose was so happy that she got all mixed up: she dropped nuts into her tea instead of lemon, said "Happy Birthday" to Mr. Pig instead of "Merry Christmas," and when it was time to go home, she put her rubbers on her wings instead of on her feet. But no one cared, they were so glad to see her back again. "And you won't fly away again, will you?" Three-Ducks asked her.

And she said, "No. One wild Christmas is enough for me. Animaltown is where *I* belong, forever and ever!"

—*from MRS. GOOSE AND THREE-DUCKS*
by Miriam Potter

The Friendly Beasts

Jesus, our brother, strong and good,
Was humbly born in a stable rude.
The friendly beasts around Him stood,
Jesus, our brother, strong and good.

"I," said the donkey, all shaggy and brown,
"I carried his mother uphill and down,
I carried her safely to Bethlehem town.
I," said the donkey, all shaggy and brown.

"I," said the cow, all white and red,
"I gave Him my manger for His bed,
I gave Him my hay to pillow His head.
I," said the cow, all white and red.

"I," said the sheep with the curly horn,
"I gave Him my wool for a blanket warm,
He wore my coat on Christmas morn.
I," said the sheep with the curly horn.

"I," said the camel, all yellow and black,
"Over the desert upon my back,
I brought Him a gift in the wise man's pack.
I," said the camel, all yellow and black.

"I," said the dove from the rafters high,
"I cooed Him to sleep so He would not cry.
We cooed Him to sleep, my mate and I.
I," said the dove from the rafters high.

So every beast, by some good spell,
In the stable dark was glad to tell
Of the gift he gave Immanuel—
The gift he gave Immanuel.

—medieval verses

Christmas Underground

The following story is from The Wind in the Willows *by Kenneth Grahame—one of the best-loved children's books of all time. The book tells of the adventures of Mole, Water Rat, Toad, Badger, and many of the other small animals that live in the rivers, woods, and fields of England.*

As the book begins, Mole is lured away from his comfortable underground home by the sociable Rat. A friendship develops that leads to wonderful and sometimes terrifying adventures. Finally Mole has forgotten all about his own home until one Christmas Eve. Suddenly Mole longs to see his old quarters. Rat suggests that they go for a visit. Mole is embarrassed to find that his old home is looking rather shabby and dusty. But Rat, as usual, finds much to be enthusiastic about.

"What a capital little house this is!" Mr. Rat called out cheerily. "So compact! So well planned! Everything here and in its place! We'll make a jolly night of it. The first thing we want is a good fire. I'll see to that—I always know where to find things. So this is the parlor? Splendid! Your own idea, those little sleeping bunks in the wall? Capital! Now, I'll fetch the wood and the coals, and you get a duster, Mole—you'll find one in the drawer of the kitchen table."

The Mole roused himself and dusted and polished with energy and heartiness, while the Rat, running to and fro with armfuls of fuel, soon had a cheerful blaze roaring up the chimney. He hailed the Mole to come and warm himself, but Mole promptly had another fit of the blues, dropping down on a couch in dark despair and burying his face in his duster.

"Rat," he moaned, "how about your supper, you poor, cold, hungry, weary animal? I've nothing to give you—nothing—not a crumb!"

"What a fellow you are for giving in!" said the Rat reproachfully. "Why, only just now I saw a sardine opener on the kitchen dresser, quite distinctly; and everybody knows that means there are sardines about somewhere in the neighborhood. Rouse yourself! Pull yourself together and come with me and forage."

They went and foraged accordingly, hunting through every cupboard and turning out every drawer. The result was not so very depressing after all, though of course it might have been better: a tin of sardines; a box of captain's biscuits, nearly full; and a German sausage encased in silver paper.

"There's a banquet for you!" observed the Rat as he arranged the table. "I know some animals who would give their ears to be sitting down to supper with us tonight! And that reminds me—what's that little door at the end of the passage? Your cellar, of course! Every luxury in this house! Just you wait a minute."

He made for the cellar door and presently reappeared, somewhat dusty,

with a bottle of beer in each paw and another under each arm. "Self-indulgent beggar you seem to be, Mole," he observed. "This is really the jolliest little place I ever was in."

Then, while the Rat busied himself fetching plates, knives and forks, and mustard, which he mixed in an egg cup, the Mole related—somewhat shyly at first—how this was planned and how that was thought out, and how that was a wonderful find and a bargain, and this other thing was bought out of a certain amount of "going without."

Rat, who was desperately hungry, strove to conceal it, nodding seriously, examining with a puckered brow, and saying "Wonderful" and "Most remarkable" at intervals.

At last the Rat succeeded in decoying him to the table and had just got seriously to work with the sardine opener when sounds were heard from the forecourt without—sounds like the scuffling of small feet in the gravel and a confused murmur of tiny voices, while broken sentences reached them: "Now, all in a line—Hold the lantern up a bit, Tommy—Clear your throats first—Where's young Bill?—Here, come on, do, we're all a-waiting—"

"What's up?" inquired the Rat, pausing in his labors.

"I think it must be the field mice," replied the Mole, with a touch of pride in his manner. "They go around carol singing regularly at this time of the year. And they never pass me over—they come to Mole End last of all. And I used to give them hot drinks, and supper sometimes, when I could afford it. It will be like old times to hear them again."

"Let's have a look at them!" cried the Rat, jumping up and running to the door.

It was a pretty sight that met their eyes when they flung the door open. In the forecourt, lit by the dim rays of a horn lantern, some eight or ten little field mice stood in a semicircle, red worsted comforters around their throats, their forepaws thrust deep into their pockets, their feet jigging for warmth. With bright beady eyes they glanced shyly at each other, sniggering a little and sniffing. As the door opened, one of the elder ones that carried the lantern was just saying, "Now, then, one, two, three!" and forthwith their shrill little voices uprose on the air, singing one of the old-time carols that their forefathers composed in fields that were held by frost, or when snowbound in chimney corners.

Villagers all, this frosty tide,
Let your doors swing open wide,
Though wind may follow, and snow beside,
Yet draw us in by your fire to bide;
Joy shall be yours in the morning!

Here we stand in the cold and the sleet,
Blowing fingers and stamping feet,
Come from far away you to greet—
You by the fire and we in the street—
Bidding you joy in the morning!

"Very well sung, boys!" cried the Rat heartily when they had finished. "And now come along in, all of you, and warm yourselves by the fire and have something hot!"

"Yes, come along, field mice," cried the Mole eagerly. "This is quite like old times. Shut the door after you. Pull up that settle to the fire. Now, you just wait a minute, while we— Oh, Ratty!" he cried in despair. "Whatever are we doing? We've nothing to give them!"

"You leave all that to me," said the masterful Rat. "Here, you with the lantern! Come over this way. I want to talk to you.

"Now, tell me, are there any shops open at this hour of the night?"

"Why, certainly, sire," replied the field mouse. "At this time of the year our shops keep open to all sorts of hours."

"Then look here!" said the Rat. "You go off at once, you and your lantern, and you get me—"

Here much muttered conversation ensued, and the Mole only heard bits of it, such as: "If you can't get it there, try somewhere else—yes, of course, homemade, no tinned stuff—well then, do the best you can!" Finally, there was a chink of coin passing from paw to paw, the field mouse was provided with an ample basket for his purchases, and off he hurried.

The rest of the field mice, perched in a row on the settle, their small legs swinging, gave themselves up to the enjoyment of the fire.

It did not take long to prepare the brew and thrust the tin heater well into the red heart of the fire. And soon every field mouse was sipping and coughing and choking and wiping his eyes and laughing and forgetting he had ever been cold in all his life.

"They act plays, too, these fellows," the Mole explained to the Rat. "Make them up all by themselves and act them afterward. And very well they do it, too!" But then the latch clicked, the door opened, and the field mouse with the lantern reappeared, staggering under the weight of his basket.

There was no more talk of playacting once the very real and solid contents of the basket had been tumbled out on the table. Under the generalship of Rat, everybody was set to do something or to fetch something. In a very few minutes supper was ready, and Mole, as he took the head of the table in a sort of dream, saw a lately barren board set

thick with savory comforts; saw his little friends' faces brighten and beam
as they fell to without delay. What a happy homecoming this had turned
out, after all! As they ate, they talked of old times, and the field mice gave
Mole the local gossip up to date, and answered as well as they could the
hundred questions he had to ask them.

They clattered off at last, very grateful and showering wishes of the
season. When the door had closed and the chink of the lanterns had died
away, Mole and Rat kicked the fire up, drew their chairs in, brewed
themselves a last nightcap of mulled ale, and discussed the events of the
long day.

—*Kenneth Grahame*

What Can I Give Him?

What can I give Him,
*   Poor as I am?*
If I were a shepherd
*   I would bring a lamb,*
If I were a wise man
*   I would do my part,*
Yet what I can I give Him—
*   Give my heart.*

—Christina Rossetti

PART THREE
The Story of the Christ Child

The Birth of Jesus

It came to pass in those days that a decree went out from Caesar Augustus, the emperor in Rome, that all the world should be taxed.

Everyone went to be taxed, each to his own city. And Joseph went up from Galilee, from the city of Nazareth, into Judea, to the city of David, which is called Bethlehem, because he was of the house and family of David, to be taxed with Mary, his wife, who was soon to have a child.

And it came to pass that while they were there, the day arrived for her child to be born. She brought forth her firstborn son and wrapped him in swaddling clothes and laid him in a manger, because there was no room for them in the inn.

There were in the same country shepherds staying in the field, keeping watch over their flocks by night. And, lo, the angel of the Lord came upon them, and the glory of the Lord shone round about them, and they were much afraid.

"Fear not," the angel said to them. "For I bring you good tidings of a great joy that is coming to all people. For to you is born this day in the city of David a Savior who is Christ the Lord. And this shall be a sign to you: You shall find the babe wrapped in swaddling clothes, lying in a manger."

And suddenly there was with the angel a multitude of the heavenly host praising God and saying:

"Glory to God in the highest, and on earth peace, good will toward men."

When the angels had gone away from them into heaven, the shepherds said to one another, "Let us go into Bethlehem and see this thing which has come to pass, which the Lord has made known to us."

They went with haste and found Mary and Joseph, and the babe lying in a manger. And when they had seen it, they made known throughout the land what they had been told concerning this child. And all who heard it marveled at the things which were told to them by the shepherds. But Mary kept all these things and pondered them in her heart.

—Luke 2

O Little Town of Bethlehem

*Phillips Brooks, a well-loved American clergyman, quickly wrote down the
words for this carol on Christmas Eve, 1868, for the children of his Sunday school
to sing at their Christmas services. The verses were inspired, it is thought,
by his trip to the Holy Land three years earlier, and his visit to Bethlehem
shortly before Christmas. Lewis Redner, the church organist, rushed to
compose the tune that night, it is told, and the hymn was
ready for the children to sing the next morning.*

Phillips Brooks   **Lewis H. Redner**

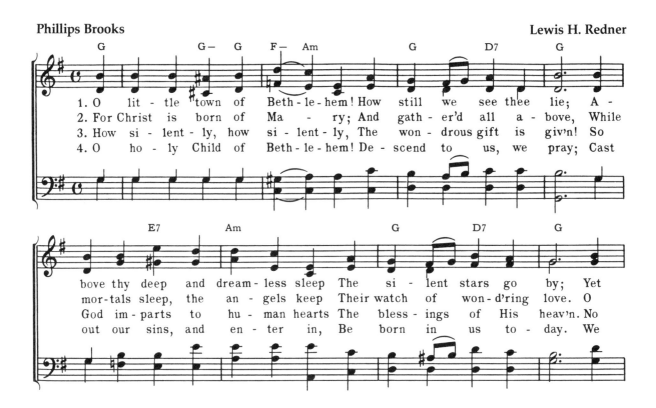

1. O lit-tle town of Beth-le-hem! How still we see thee lie; A-
2. For Christ is born of Ma - ry; And gath-er'd all a-bove, While
3. How si-lent-ly, how si-lent-ly, The won-drous gift is giv'n! So
4. O ho-ly Child of Beth-le-hem! De-scend to us, we pray; Cast

bove thy deep and dream-less sleep The si - lent stars go by; Yet
mor-tals sleep, the an-gels keep Their watch of won-d'ring love. O
God im-parts to hu-man hearts The bless-ings of His heav'n. No
out our sins, and en-ter in, Be born in us to - day. We

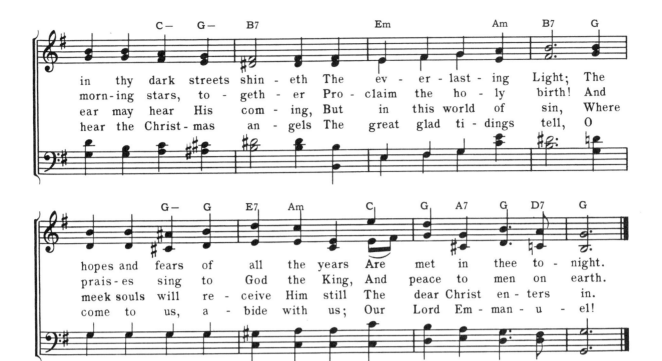

in thy dark streets shin - eth The ev - er - last - ing Light; The
morn-ing stars, to - geth - er Pro - claim the ho - ly birth! And
ear may hear His com - ing, But in this world of sin, Where
hear the Christ - mas an - gels The great glad ti - dings tell, O

hopes and fears of all the years Are met in thee to - night.
prais - es sing to God the King, And peace to men on earth.
meek souls will re - ceive Him still The dear Christ en - ters in.
come to us, a - bide with us; Our Lord Em - man - u - el!

The Christmas Spider

The grey spider worked very hard every day making long strands of silk that he wove into a web in which he caught troublesome flies. But he noticed that every one turned away from him because, they said, he was so unpleasant to look at with his long, crooked legs and furry body. Of course the grey spider didn't believe that, because he had only the kindliest feelings for everybody. One day when he was crossing the stream he looked into the water. There he saw himself as he really was.

"Oh," he thought, "I *am* very unpleasant to look at. I shall keep out of people's way." He was very sad and hid himself in the darkest corner of the stable. There he again began to work as he always had, weaving long strands of silk into webs and catching flies. The donkey and the ox and the sheep who lived in the stable thanked him for his kindness, because now they were no longer bothered with the buzzing flies. That made the spider very happy.

One night, exactly at midnight, the spider was awakened by a brilliant light. He looked about and saw that the light came from the manger where a tiny Child lay on the hay. The stable was filled with glory, and over the Child bent a beautiful mother. Behind her stood a man with a staff in his hand, and the ox and the donkey and all the white sheep were down on their knees.

Suddenly a gust of cold wind swept through the stable and the Baby began to weep from the cold. The mother bent over Him but could not cover Him enough to keep Him warm. The little spider took his silken web and laid it at Mary's feet (for it was Mary) and Mary took up the web and covered the Baby with it. It was soft as thistledown and as warm as wool. The Child stopped his crying and smiled at the little grey spider.

Then Mary said, "Little grey spider, for this great gift to the Babe you may have anything you wish."

"Most of all," said the spider, "I wish to be beautiful."

"That I cannot give you," Mary answered. "You must stay as you are for as long as you live. But this I grant you. Whenever any one sees a spider at evening, he will count it a good omen, and it shall bring him good fortune."

This made the spider very happy, and to this day, on Christmas Eve, we cover the Christmas Tree with "angel's hair" in memory of the little grey spider and his silken web.

—a Polish folktale retold by Marguerite de Angeli

The Visit of the Wise Men

Now, when Jesus was born in Bethlehem of Judea, in the days of Herod the king, there came wise men from the east to Jerusalem, asking: "Where is he that is born King of the Jews? For we have seen his star in the east and are come to worship him."

When Herod the king heard these things, he was troubled, and all Jerusalem with him. And when he had gathered all the chief priests and scribes of the people together, he asked them where Christ should be born. "In Bethlehem of Judea," they said. "For thus it is written by the prophet:

'And you, Bethlehem, in the land of Judah,
are not the least among the princes of Judah.
For out of you shall come a Governor
that shall rule my people Israel.'"

Then Herod sent secretly for the wise men and asked them what time the star had appeared. And he sent them to Bethlehem, saying, "Go and search carefully for the young child, and when you have found him, bring me word, that I may come and worship him also."

When they had heard the king, they departed. And, lo, the star which they saw in the east went before them till it came and stood over the place where the young child was. When they saw the star, they rejoiced with great joy. And when they came into the house, they saw the young child with Mary, his mother, and they fell down and worshiped him and presented gifts to him: gold, frankincense, and myrrh. And being warned by God in a dream that they should not return to Herod, they departed and returned to their own country by another way.

—*Matthew 2*

We Three Kings of Orient Are

Carol singing began fairly late in America, for the Pilgrim Fathers frowned upon Christmas celebrations of any kind. This carol was written in 1857, both words and music by the Rev. John Henry Hopkins. In it each of the kings of the Orient tells of the gift he has brought to the Christ Child.

John H. Hopkins

John H. Hopkins

All
1. We three kings of Orient are; Bearing gifts we traverse a-

Melchior
2. Born a King on Beth-le-hem's plain, Gold I bring, to crown Him a-

Caspar
3. Frank-in-cense to of-fer have I, In-cense owns a De-i-ty

Balthazar
4. Myrrh is mine, its bit-ter per-fume Breathes a life of gath-er-ing

All
5. Glo-rious now be-hold Him a-rise, King and God and sac-ri-

far, Field and foun-tain, moor and moun-tain, Fol-low-ing yon-der star.

gain, King for-ev-er, ceas-ing nev-er, O-ver us all to reign.

nigh, Pray'r and prais-ing, all men rais-ing, Wor-ship Him, God most High.

gloom; Sor-row-ing, sigh-ing, bleed-ing, dy-ing, Seal'd in the stone-cold tomb.

fice; Al-le-lu-ia, Al-le-lu-ia, Earth to the heav'ns re-plies.

CHORUS

O star of won-der, star of night, Star with roy-al beau-ty bright,

West-ward lead-ing, still pro-ceed-ing, Guide us to Thy per-fect light.

La Befana

In Italy long ago there was an old woman who lived in a lonely cottage. One day she was just taking her broom from its corner to sweep the rough wooden floor when she heard a knock on the door. Opening the door a narrow crack, she peered out. There stood three foreign gentlemen in splendid robes. They were searching for a newborn child, they said, a great king, who was in Bethlehem. Could she show them the way?

The old woman knew nothing about a place called Bethlehem. She was tired, and she still had not finished her household chores. So she shook her head and offered the gentlemen no help, closed the door abruptly, and went back to her sweeping. Only once did she look out of the window. The three strange men were moving over the brow of a hill. Then they disappeared from sight.

All that evening the old woman could not help thinking about the visitors and about the child they were going to see. And the more she thought, the more ashamed she was of her rudeness. She made up her mind that, in the morning, she would go in search of the three men and the child.

When dawn broke, she was already on her way, wrapped in a red shawl and heavy cloak. In one hand she carried her broom, and with the other hand she led a donkey. Both her shoulder pack and donkey were laden with gifts. But search as she might, through the snows of winter and the heat of summer, she never found the three men or the child.

In Italy they say that to this day La Befana walks the weary miles, and her search is never ending. There is also a tradition that on January 5, the eve of Epiphany, she leaves gifts from her pack for good children, and for naughty children she leaves birch rods and ashes. The woman's name, Befana, comes from *Epifania*, the holiday on which the three kings found the babe in Bethlehem and presented their gifts of gold, frankincense, and myrrh.

—a Christmas legend from Italy,
retold by Lillian Lewicki

The Inn That Missed Its Chance

(The Landlord Speaks, A.D. 28)

What could be done? The inn was full of folks!
His honor, Marcus Lucius, and his scribes
Who made the census: honorable men
From farthest Galilee, come hitherward
To be enrolled; high ladies and their lords;
The rich, the rabbis, such a noble throng
As Bethlehem had never seen before
And may not see again. And there they were,
Close-herded with their servants, till the inn
Was like a hive at swarming-time, and I
Was fairly crazed among them.

              Could I know
That *they* were so important? Just the two,
No servants, just a workman sort of man,
Leading a donkey, and his wife thereon
Drooping and pale,—I saw them not myself,
My servants must have driven them away;
But had I seen them,—how was I to know?
Were inns to welcome stragglers, up and down
In all our towns from Beersheba to Dan,
Till He should come? And how were men to know?

There was a sign, they say, a heavenly light
Resplendent: but I had no time for stars,
And there were songs of angels in the air
Out on the hills; but how was I to hear
Amid the thousand clamors of an inn?
Of course, if I had known them, who they were,
And who was He that should be born that night,—
For now I learn that they will make Him King,
A second David, who will ransom us
From these Philistine Romans,—who but He
That feeds an army with a loaf of bread,
And if a soldier falls, He touches him
And up he leaps, uninjured?—Had I known,
I would have turned the whole inn upside down,
His honor, Marcus Lucius, and the rest,
And sent them all to stables, had I known.

So you have seen Him, stranger, and perhaps
Again may see Him? Prithee say for me,
I did not know; and if He comes again
As He will surely come, with retinue,
And banners, and an army, tell my Lord
That all my inn is His to make amends.

Alas! Alas! to miss a chance like that!
This inn that might be chief among them all,
The birthplace of Messiah,—had I known!

—*Amos Russel Wells*

New England

The Pilgrims were pious,
The Pilgrims were brave,
They had lands to conquer,
And souls to save.
They were busy and bold
  And worthy, very.
But they didn't hold
  With making merry.
Though they loved the Lord,
Historians say
They never rejoiced
On Christmas Day.

For twenty-two years
From Plymouth's founding
They kept the carols
From ever sounding.
Their lights didn't shine,
Their bells didn't jingle.

They shut their chimneys
On good Kris Kringle,
And termed it pagan,
And thought it shocking
To hang a wreath
Or a Christmas stocking.

No cakes, no presents,
No Christmas mirth,
No "Alleluia!"
No "Peace on earth,"
Nothing but sermons
At Sunday meeting,
And a stern rebuke
For Christmas greeting.
Oh, aren't you glad
That you weren't alive
In sixteen-twenty
Or twenty-five?

—Phyllis McGinley

70

PART FOUR
The Wonder of Christmas Past

Christmas Eve
on the Battlefront

The story below comes from a book called The Singing Tree *by Kate Seredy. The author was born in Budapest, Hungary, where she worked as a nurse in military hospitals during World War I. The book tells about the adventures of two cousins, Kate and Jancsi, who live on a farm in the Hungarian countryside. In the excerpt reprinted here, Jancsi's father has been sent home from the army to recuperate from wounds received while fighting against Russian troops. On Christmas Eve he tells his family the strange tale of a miracle that took place just a year earlier on the Russian–Hungarian battlefront.*

Father had saved one story for Christmas Eve and told it while the candles were burning on the tree. The faint sound of village church bells coming across the plains made his story of another Christmas Eve sound like a song of hope, hope that maybe kindness and love of peace would be strong enough to stop the war soon. For the first time he spoke of things like offensive, march, trenches, shellfire, but the dark picture these words created was only a backdrop against which his story of human souls shone all the brighter.

"Last Christmas Eve," he began, "we had received orders to be prepared for a surprise attack against the Russians. Our trenches had been under heavy fire for days; we had either to retreat or to advance, and those who plan the moves of war decided on an advance.

"We had been waiting for hours, crouching against the walls of our trenches, when the word came: 'Go.'

"We crept out into the snow, countless silent dark shapes against the whiteness, and ran to the sunken road which lay between our lines and the mountainside where the Russian trenches were. Shells screamed overhead and burst behind us, drowning out all noise we might have made, and when we reached the road, whispered orders from the Captain scurried down the line like mice: 'Advance along the road. Don't dare make a sound or strike a light.'

"We tramped in knee-deep snow, skirting the friendly hillside that sheltered us from the fire, stealing toward the Russians. And then, just ahead of me I saw a boy kneel in the snow before a wayside crucifix and light a candle. It flickered in the still air, casting a feeble light on the

73

image of Christ above it. 'Oh, Lord,' the man next to me sighed, reaching into his knapsack for a candle. Others had seen the glowing light, and as I looked around I saw that more and more candles were lighted all around. A whisper spread, like the order from the Captain, from mouth to mouth, only this was not an order from the Captain. 'Light a candle for Christmas Eve,' men whispered and their very words seemed to turn into tiny stars as dozens and dozens, then hundreds of candles came forth from the knapsacks to be lighted and stuck in the snow. The hillside now was one glow of light and the crucifix was bright with an unearthly brightness. We were a target for the Russian guns, but we never gave it a thought. For a little while we were lost in prayer, until one of the men cried: 'They have stopped firing. Look!'

"Across the valley, on the hillside where the Russians were entrenched, a few small flames began to tremble, then more and more. Candles, hundreds of them, thousands, one for every gun that now was silent.

Around me men began to sing 'Holy Night, Silent Night,' and from across the valley the song came back to us a thousandfold. Behind the lines so facing each other, the guns had ceased to roar and no more shells were screaming between men and the stars. Perhaps the Christ Child had walked between the lines and while He walked, peace had stayed the guns."

Father had finished his story. Kate sighed, a long, tremulous sigh: "Oh, that was beautiful! What happened after?" Father shivered as if with the cold and rose to close the door. Only then did he answer:

"The candles burned down, Kate, and…darkness closed in again. Let those who made the war hear the story of what happened after. Let them see…." He lifted his arm and covered his eyes, but when he looked up his face was smiling. "Oh, no. This is another Christmas Eve, and the Christ Child must not find hate in our hearts."

—Kate Seredy

Good King Wenceslas

An old Bohemian legend tells of Wenzel the Holy, Ruler of Bohemia from A.D. 928 to 935, and of his many good deeds and kind acts to the poor. He is especially known for the generosity he showed during one particular Feast of St. Stephen, held on December 26.

Traditional

Arranged by Norman Lloyd

1. Good King Wen - ces - las look'd out, On the feast of Ste - phen,
2. "Hith - er, page, and stand by me, If thou knows't it tell - ing,
3. "Bring me flesh, and bring me wine, Bring me pine - logs hith - er:
4. "Sire, the night is dark - er now, And the wind grows strong - er;
5. In his mas - ter's steps he trod, Where the snow lay dint - ed;

When the snow lay round - a - bout, Deep and crisp and e - ven.
Yon - der peas - ant, who is he? Where and what his dwell - ing?"
Thou and I shall see him dine, When we bear them thith - er."
Fails my heart I know not how; I can go no long - er."
Heat was in the ver - y sod Which the Saint had print - ed.

Bright - ly shone the moon that night, Though the frost was cru - el,
"Sire, he lives a good league hence, Un - der - neath the moun - tain,
Page and mon - arch, forth they went, Forth they went to - geth - er;
"Mark my foot - steps, my good page, Tread thou in them bold - ly;
There - fore, Chris - tian men, be sure, Wealth or rank pos - sess - ing,

When a poor man came in sight, Gath - 'ring win - ter fu - el.
Right a - gainst the for - est fence, By Saint Ag - nes' foun - tain."
Through the rude wind's wild la - ment And the bit - ter weath - er.
Thou shalt find the win - ter's rage Freeze thy blood less cold - ly."
Ye who now will bless the poor, Shall your - selves find bless - ing.

O Christmas Tree!

The Christmas tree comes to us from Germany. There are many beautiful legends about its origin.

One tells that on the first Christmas Eve, the winter trees bloomed as if it were springtime.

Another legend says that Martin Luther, the stern reformer, lighted candles on a small fir tree to show his little son how the starry heavens must have looked on that first silent Christmas Eve.

Still another legend tells of a wandering child who was taken into the home of a poor forester, fed, and tucked into a warm bed. In the morning, the child was seen to be the Christ Child Himself.

Before He left the humble cottage, He put an evergreen twig in the ground and promised that it would grow to be a tall tree that would—ever after—bring plenty to the forester and his family.

—Kathryn Jackson

Christmas Stockings

The custom of hanging stockings on Christmas Eve stems from an old legend as well. It is said that St. Nicholas, then a kindly Greek bishop, took pity on a poor man whose three comely daughters could not marry because he had no gold for their dowries.

By night, the good bishop dropped a purse full of gold down the man's chimney. It landed, by chance, in one of the stockings the eldest daughter had hung up to dry. Now she could be married.

Soon the next daughter, then the next, hung up a stocking for St. Nicholas to fill with gold.

He did, and in turn, they were married to good men, too.

In time, because of this legend, children began hanging up their stockings—hoping to find them filled with gifts.

—*Kathryn Jackson*

79

A Miserable, Merry Christmas

Lincoln Steffens was born in San Francisco in 1866 and spent most of his boyhood years on a small California ranch near Sacramento. Although he later became famous for his newspaper articles, he never forgot the youthful joys of riding horseback with his cowboy friends. The first part of the Autobiography of Lincoln Steffens, *published in 1931, provides a classic picture of what it was like to be a boy in California during the 1870s, when the glamor of pioneer days had not yet faded. In the excerpt that follows, Steffens tells about the Christmas when he wanted a pony more than anything else in the world. As you read the story, you will discover why that particular Christmas turned out to be both the best and the worst Christmas of his entire life.*

My father's business seems to have been one of slow but steady growth. He and his local partner, Llewelen Tozer, were devoted to their families and to "the store," which grew with the town.

As the store made money and I was getting through the primary school, my father bought a lot uptown, at Sixteenth and K Streets, and built us a "big" house. It was off the line of the city's growth, but it was near a new grammar school for me and my sisters, who were coming along fast after me. This interested the family, not me. They were always talking about school; they had not had much of it themselves, and they thought they had missed something.

What interested me in our new neighborhood was not the school, nor the room I was to have in the house all to myself, but the stable which was built back of the house. My father let me direct the making of a stall, a little smaller than the other stalls, for my pony, and I prayed and hoped and my sister Lou believed that that meant that I would get the pony, perhaps for Christmas. I pointed out to her that there were three other stalls and no horses at all. This I said in order that she should answer it. She could not. My father, sounded, said that some day we might have horses and a cow;

meanwhile a stable added to the value of a house. "Some day" is a pain to a boy who lives in and knows only "now." My good little sisters, to comfort me, remarked that Christmas was coming, but Christmas was always coming and grown-ups were always talking about it, asking you what you wanted and then giving you what they wanted you to have. Though everybody knew what I wanted, I told them all again. My mother knew that I told God, too, every night. I wanted a pony, and to make sure that they understood, I declared that I wanted nothing else.

"Nothing but a pony?" my father asked.

"Nothing," I said.

"Not even a pair of high boots?"

That was hard. I did want boots, but I stuck to the pony. "No, not even boots."

"Nor candy? There ought to be something to fill your stocking with, and Santa Claus can't put a pony into a stocking."

That was true, and he couldn't lead a pony down the chimney either. But no. "All I want is a pony," I said. "If I can't have a pony, give me nothing, nothing."

Now I had been looking myself for the pony I wanted, going to sales stables, inquiring of horsemen, and I had seen several that would do. My father let me "try" them. I tried so many ponies that I was learning fast to sit a horse. I chose several, but my father always found some fault with them. I was in despair. When Christmas was at hand I had given up all hope of a pony, and on Christmas Eve I hung up my stocking along with my sisters', of whom, by the way, I now had three. They were so happy that Christmas Eve that I caught some of their merriment. I speculated on what I'd get; I hung up the biggest stocking I had, and we all went reluctantly to bed to wait till morning. Not to sleep; not right away. We were told that we must not only sleep promptly, we must not wake up till seven-thirty the next morning—or if we did, we must not go to the fireplace for our Christmas. Impossible.

We did sleep that night, but we woke up at six A.M. We lay in our beds and debated through the open doors whether to obey till, say, half-past six. Then we bolted. I don't know who started it, but there was a rush. We all disobeyed; we raced to disobey and get first to the fireplace in the front room downstairs. And there they were, the gifts, all sorts of wonderful

things, mixed-up piles of presents; only, as I disentangled the mess, I saw that my stocking was empty; it hung limp; not a thing in it; and under and around it—nothing. My sisters had knelt down, each by her pile of gifts; they were squealing with delight, till they looked up and saw me standing there in my nightgown with nothing. They left their piles to come to me and look with me at my empty place. Nothing. They felt my stocking: nothing.

I don't remember whether I cried at that moment, but my sisters did. They ran with me back to my bed, and there we all cried till I became indignant. That helped some. I got up, dressed, and driving my sisters away, I went alone out into the yard, down to the stable, and there, all by myself, I wept. My mother came out to me by and by; she found me in my pony stall, sobbing on the floor, and she tried to comfort me. But I heard my father outside; he had come part way with her, and she was having some sort of angry quarrel with him. She tried to comfort me; besought me to come to breakfast. I could not; I wanted no comfort and no breakfast. She left me and went on into the house with sharp words for my father.

I don't know what kind of a breakfast the family had. My sisters said it was "awful." They were ashamed to enjoy their own toys. They came to me, and I was rude. I ran away from them. I went around to the front of the house, sat down on the steps, and, the crying over, I ached. I was wronged,

I was hurt—I can feel now what I felt then, and I am sure that if one could see the wounds upon our hearts, there would be found still upon mine a scar from that terrible Christmas morning. And my father, the practical joker, he must have been hurt, too, a little. I saw him looking out of the window. He was watching me or something for an hour or two, drawing back the curtain ever so little lest I catch him, but I saw his face, and I think I can see now the anxiety upon it, the worried impatience.

After—I don't know how long—surely an hour or two—I was brought to the climax of my agony by the sight of a man riding a pony down the street, a pony and a brand-new saddle; the most beautiful saddle I ever saw, and it was a boy's saddle; the man's feet were not in the stirrups; his legs were too long. The outfit was perfect; it was the realization of all my dreams, the answer to all my prayers. A fine new bridle, with a light curb bit. And the pony! As he drew near, I saw that the pony was really a small horse, what we called an Indian pony, a bay, with black mane and tail, and one white foot and a white star on his forehead. For such a horse as that I would have given, I could have forgiven, anything.

But the man, a disheveled fellow with a blackened eye and a fresh-cut face, came along, reading the numbers on the houses, and, as my hopes—my impossible hopes—rose, he looked at our door and passed by, he and the pony, and the saddle and the bridle. Too much. I fell upon the steps, and having wept before, I broke now into such a flood of tears that I was a floating wreck when I heard a voice.

"Say, kid," it said, "do you know a boy named Lennie Steffens?"

I looked up. It was the man on the pony, back again, at our horse block.

"Yes," I spluttered through my tears. "That's me."

"Well," he said, "then this is your horse. I've been looking all over for you and your house. Why don't you put your number where it can be seen?"

"Get down," I said, running out to him.

He went on saying something about "ought to have got here at seven o'clock; told me to bring the nag here and tie him to your post and leave him for you."

He got down, and he boosted me up to the saddle. He offered to fit the stirrups to me, but I didn't want him to. I wanted to ride.

"What's the matter with you?" he said, angrily. "What you crying for? Don't you like the horse? He's a dandy, this horse. I know him of old. He's fine at cattle; he'll drive 'em alone."

I hardly heard, I could scarcely wait, but he persisted. He adjusted the stirrups, and then, finally, off I rode, slowly, at a walk, so happy, so thrilled, that I did not know what I was doing. I did not look back at the house or the man, I rode off up the street, taking note of everything—of the reins, of the pony's long mane, of the carved leather saddle. I had never seen anything so beautiful. And mine! I was going to ride up past Miss Kay's house. But I noticed on the horn of the saddle some stains like rain-drops, so I turned and trotted home, not to the house but to the stable. There was the family, father, mother, sisters, all working for me, all happy. They had been putting in place the tools of my new business: blankets, currycomb, brush, pitchfork—everything, and there was hay in the loft.

"What did you come back so soon for?" somebody asked. "Why didn't you go on riding?"

I pointed to the stains. "I wasn't going to get my new saddle rained on," I said. And my father laughed. "It isn't raining," he said. "Those are not rain-drops."

"They are tears," my mother gasped, and she gave my father a look which sent him off to the house. Worse still, my mother offered to wipe away the tears still running out of my eyes. I gave her such a look as she had given him, and she went off after my father, drying her own tears. My sisters remained and we all unsaddled the pony, put on his halter, led him to his stall, tied and fed him. It began really to rain; so all the rest of that memorable day we curried and combed that pony. The girls plaited his mane, forelock, and tail, while I pitchforked hay to him and curried and brushed, curried and brushed. For a change we brought him out to drink; we led him up and down, blanketed like a race-horse; we took turns at that. But the best, the most inexhaustible fun, was to clean him. When we went reluctantly to our midday Christmas dinner, we all smelt of horse, and my sisters had to wash their faces and hands. I was asked to, but I wouldn't, till

my mother bade me look in the mirror. Then I washed up—quick. My face was caked with the muddy lines of tears that had coursed over my cheeks to my mouth. Having washed away that shame, I ate my dinner, and as I ate I grew hungrier and hungrier. It was my first meal that day, and as I filled up on the turkey and the stuffing, the cranberries and the pies, the fruit and the nuts—as I swelled, I could laugh. My mother said I still choked and sobbed now and then, but I laughed, too; I saw and enjoyed my sisters' presents till—I had to go out and attend to my pony, who was there, really and truly there, the promise, the beginning, of a happy double life. And—I went and looked to make sure—there was the saddle, too, and the bridle.

But that Christmas, which my father had planned so carefully, was it the best or the worst I ever knew? He often asked me that; I never could answer as a boy. I think now that it was both. It covered the whole distance from broken-hearted misery to bursting happiness—too fast. A grown-up could hardly have stood it.

—*Lincoln Steffens*

A Visit From Saint Nicholas

'Twas the night before Christmas and all through
  the house,
Not a creature was stirring, not even a mouse.
The stockings were hung by the chimney with care
In hopes that Saint Nicholas soon would be there.
The children were nestled all snug in their beds,
While visions of sugarplums danced in their heads;
And Mamma in her kerchief, and I in my cap,
Had just settled down for a long winter's nap,
When out on the lawn there arose such a clatter,
I sprang from the bed to see what was the matter.
Away to the window I flew like a flash,
Tore open the shutters and threw up the sash.
The moon on the breast of the new-fallen snow
Gave the luster of midday to objects below,

When what to my wondering eyes should appear
But a miniature sleigh and eight tiny reindeer,
With a little old driver so lively and quick,
I knew in a moment it must be Saint Nick.
More rapid than eagles his coursers they came,
And he whistled and shouted and called them by name:
"Now, Dasher! Now, Dancer! Now, Prancer! Now, Vixen!
On, Comet! On, Cupid! On, Donder and Blitzen!
To the top of the porch! To the top of the wall!
Now dash away, dash away, dash away, all!"
As dry leaves that before the wild hurricane fly,
When they meet with an obstacle, mount to the sky,
So up to the housetop the coursers they flew,
With the sleigh full of toys and Saint Nicholas, too.
And then, in a twinkling, I heard on the roof
The prancing and pawing of each tiny hoof.
As I drew in my head and was turning around,

Down the chimney Saint Nicholas came with a bound.
He was dressed all in fur from his head to his foot,
And his clothes were all tarnished with ashes and soot.
A bundle of toys he had flung on his back,
And he looked like a peddler just opening his pack.
His eyes, how they twinkled! His dimples, how merry!
His cheeks were like roses, his nose like a cherry!
His droll little mouth was drawn up like a bow,
And the beard on his chin was as white as the snow.
The stump of a pipe he held tight in his teeth,
And the smoke it encircled his head like a wreath.
He had a broad face and a round little belly
That shook, when he laughed, like a bowl full of jelly.
He was chubby and plump, a right jolly old elf,

And I laughed when I saw him, in spite of myself.
A wink of his eye and a twist of his head
Soon gave me to know I had nothing to dread.
He spoke not a word but went straight to his work,
And filled all the stockings, then turned with a jerk,
And laying a finger aside of his nose
And giving a nod, up the chimney he rose.
He sprang to his sleigh, to his team gave a whistle,
And away they all flew like the down of a thistle.
But I heard him exclaim, ere he drove out of sight,
"Happy Christmas to all, and to all a good night!"

—*Clement C. Moore*